NEW IN AT YOUR LIBRARY!

WOLVES

Emily Grrrabbit

Burrow WOLVES and many other rip-roaring tails at your local library NOW!

TW🦉 HOOTS

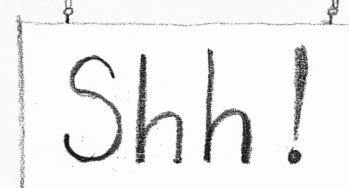

Rabbit went to the library.
He chose a book about . . .

WOLVES

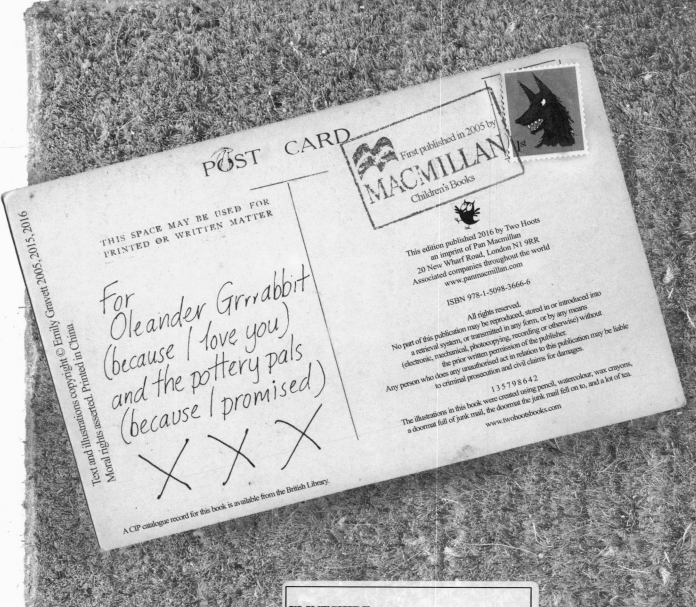

POST CARD

First published in 2005 by
MACMILLAN
Children's Books

THIS SPACE MAY BE USED FOR
PRINTED OR WRITTEN MATTER

Text and illustrations copyright © Emily Gravett 2005, 2015, 2016
Moral rights asserted. Printed in China.

For
Oleander Grrrabbit
(because I love you)
and the pottery pals
(because I promised)
X X X

A CIP catalogue record for this book is available from the British Library.

This edition published 2016 by Two Hoots
an imprint of Pan Macmillan
20 New Wharf Road, London N1 9RR
Associated companies throughout the world
www.panmacmillan.com

ISBN 978-1-5098-3666-6

135798642

The illustrations in this book were created using pencil, watercolour, wax crayons,
a doormat full of junk mail, the doormat the junk mail fell on to, and a lot of tea.
www.twohootsbooks.com

WOLVES

GREY WOLVES live in packs of between two and ten animals.

They can survive almost anywhere:
from the Arctic Circle . . .

. . . to the outskirts of towns and villages.

In some areas wolves have retreated
to places where fewer people live,
such as forests and woodland.

They have sharp claws . . .

. . . bushy tails . . .

. . . and dense fur, which harbours fleas and ticks.

An adult wolf has 42 teeth.
Its jaws are twice as powerful
as those of a large dog.

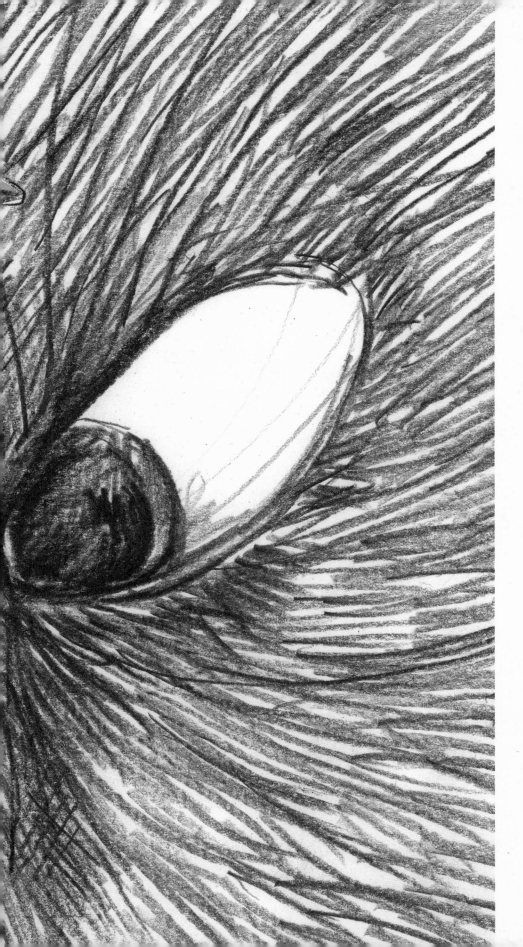

Wolves eat mainly
meat. They hunt
large prey such
as deer, bison and
moose.

They also enjoy
smaller mammals,
like beavers, voles
and . . .

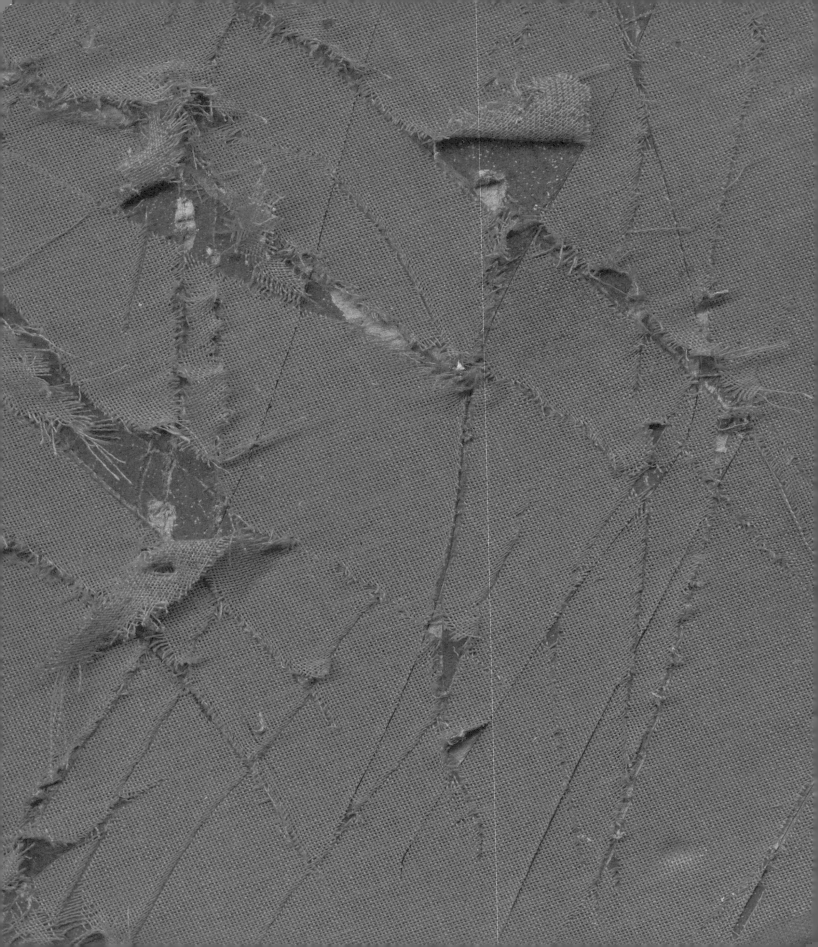

. . . rabbits.

The author would like to point out
that no rabbits were eaten during
the making of this book.
It is a work of fiction.
And so, for more sensitive readers,
here is an alternative ending.

Luckily this wolf was a vegetarian, so they
shared a jam sandwich, became the best of
friends, and lived happily ever after.

Burrowed Wok

Carrotenese Take Away

43 RABBIT RUN · THE HUTCH
DITCHLING ROAD · SALAD PATCHAM
TELEPHONE ORDERS WELCOME

TELEPHONE 260497

DELIVERY SERVICE AVAILABLE
7 EVENINGS A WEEK
From: 5.30pm – 11.00pm
Within 3 Miles £1.00, 4-5 Miles £1.50

FREE **Lawn Crackers**
on orders over £10

FREE **Morning Dew**
on orders over £30

· **OPENING HOURS** ·
Monday - Thursday   5pm - 11.30pm
Friday - Saturday   5pm - 12 Midnight
Sunday   5pm - 11.00pm

RABBIT MAIL
POSTAGE PAID
HQ 6733
GREAT BURROW

Angora Organics
GARDENING CATALOGUE
Every seed you need for the perfect patch.

G. RABBIT
LANE'S END BURROW
THE LONG FIELD
NIBBLESWICK

3

Seven little rabbits gnawing on sticks;
One turned out to be a snake and then there were six.

Six little rabbits spied honey in a hive;
One went in to get some and then there were five.

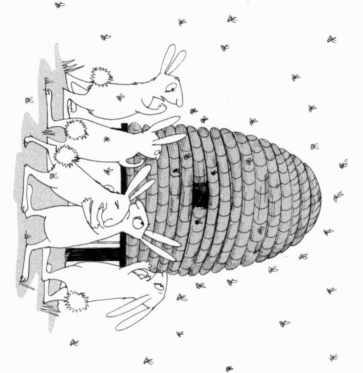

Five little rabbits, each with a lucky paw;
One was *not* so lucky and then there were four.

Four little rabbits hid behind a tree;
A wolf was on the other side and then there were three.

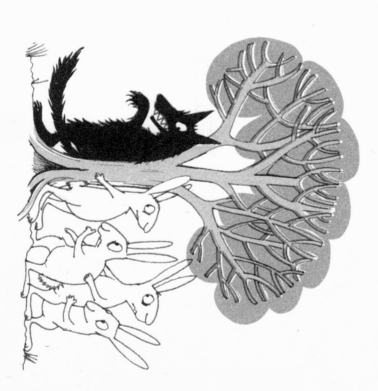

4

Nine little rabbits looked up and saw the weight;

One was looking at the ground and then there were eight.

Eight little rabbits think their burrow's heaven;

One went outside alone and then there were seven.

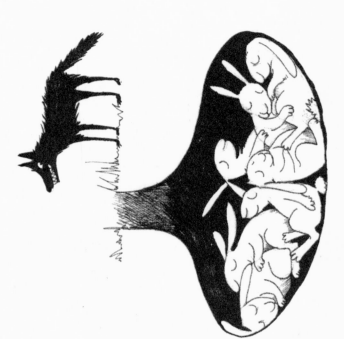

Three little rabbits sniffed at the stew;

One fell in and then there were two.

Ten little rabbits hopped out to dine;

One got caught in a net and then there were nine.

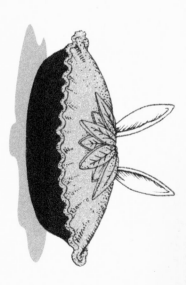

Two little rabbits left. Now we're nearly done;

One became a rabbit pie and then there was . . .

One little rabbit all by himself;

Went to the library and chose a book from the shelf . . . .

A Wolf's Tail

10 Little Rabbits

Fold
along
the
dotted
line ►

Cut along dashed line ✂

**Ten little rabbits hop out to dine.
But are they alone?**

Little Nipper Press

Dear Reader,
After all that destruction,
here is a little CONSTRUCTION.
A chance to make your very
own book.
Cut out the next 2 pages
where marked, and fold
in half. Sew or staple
the pages together to find
out WHY rabbit burrowed 'WOLVES' from the librar

To/
THE READERS
WHERE-EVER THEY MAY BE
WITH LOVE

Emily Gravett